I0749201

THE FISH'S DREAM

TAHIR SHAH

THE FISH'S DREAM

A Teaching Story

TAHIR SHAH

MMXXIV

Secretum Mundi Publishing Ltd
124 City Road
London
EC1V 2NX
United Kingdom

www.secretum-mundi.com
info@secretum-mundi.com

First published by Secretum Mundi Publishing Ltd, 2024
A version of this story originally appeared in *Scorpion Soup* by Tahir Shah, 2013

THE FISH'S DREAM

A CIP catalogue record for this title is available from the British Library.

ISBN 978-1-915876-10-2

VERSION 08042024

Visit the author's website:
Tahirshah.com

Only the most foolish fish die of thirst.

Kenyan saying

Teaching Stories

When I was small, I was told stories from morning till night.

I was told stories about genies and witches and about great birds that could carry away elephants on their wings… and stories about distant kingdoms and magical lands ruled by warrior kings.

I was told stories of good and bad… stories of hope and others of despair.

I was even told stories about stories.

And all the while, I listened, amazed.

The more I listened, the more my mind worked… and the more I came to understand that these stories had a power about them, a secret lifeblood all of their own.

They were magical instruments, machineries that could alter states of mind and change the way we think.

But most importantly of all, stories can teach us, without us realizing that they are doing so at all.

Part of the default programming of man, stories are within us all.

Born into us, they make us who we are – they make us human.

Since earliest childhood, I have feasted on stories as a way of learning about the world, and learning about myself. They have been my dictionary and my encyclopaedia, my classroom, my guide, and my very best friend.

To descend down through the layers of stories is to be reborn, into a dominion of fantasy – one touched by real magic.

Pre-eminent within the great treasuries of tales, it is teaching stories like this one that have shown me the path to follow beyond the next horizon, and have made me the man I am.

Tahir Shah

Long before the earth was hard or before the seas were wet, there was an immense temple in which the gods of the universe resided.

Reclining on great golden diwans,
they would dispense wisdom to one
another through days and long nights.

And they would act with purity – a purity of spirit never to be known in the mortal world, a world that was to come.

In the centre of the temple was a sacred altar on which was kept a single volume. Bound in flaming-red cloth, this book had been written before the Conquest of Nepsis, at a time when good was bad and bad was good.

Along the spine of the volume
were inscribed the words:
The Book of Pure Thoughts.

It was by this teaching that the gods lived,
and by which they were to counsel
the rogue legions of mankind.

The Book of Pure Thoughts explained that, one day, long into the future, one of the gods would descend, and he would be known as Opee, the Divine One. Until that day, the earth would be in a state of limbo.

The era before this celestial arrival was
to be known as the Time of Solitude.

In this age, there was nothing that we know now – none of the trappings of civilization, and no fragments of the natural world.

The only exception was a fish.
A beautiful rainbow-coloured fish.

But because there was still no water,
the fish floated through the universe,
sucking its cheeks in and out.

Waiting.

It waited and waited…

… and waited and waited – for another form of life to join it, or for the seas to be created so that it might take a swim.

More millennia passed
than were ever recorded.

The fish found himself to be tremendously fatigued by his predicament. He longed for a river, a sea, or an ocean to explore, and he sang a song of solitude to the empty space around him.

With each moment that passed, the fish became
a little sadder and a little more forlorn,
his song desolate beyond words.

And this went on for an eternity, until the Protector of All Things could stand it no longer. Summoning his power, he sent the great rainbow fish a gift.

The gift of imagination.

All of a sudden, the rainbow-coloured fish
could conjure exotic dreams.

He found that by clearing his mind, he could create entire seascapes populated with other fish and sea creatures, and that he could imagine the smallest details of each one.

As the centuries slipped by, the fish learned to hone and control his imagination, and he became expert at summoning the most amazing things to mind.

He no longer needed a world, or friends, or water, and felt quite content by being entertained within the limits of his mind.

One day, although there still were no days, the fish woke up with a start. He was floating in emptiness as he had always done, but something was making him feel warm inside.

A story…

There was a miser in Persia who was so greedy that he never spent any money at all.

He grew all the food he needed on a patch of bare ground behind his ramshackle home, and he wore clothes he found in dustbins. He had no use for a horse because he pulled the cart he had built with his own callused hands.

People thereabouts used to shun him because he smelled so bad, and they would run away when he drew near.

As time went on, the miser became mute or, rather, he didn't speak, because he was so tight-fisted that he regarded talking to others as an extravagance he simply couldn't afford.

The miser would make sculptures out of scraps of wood he collected in a nearby forest and sell them in the market.

Feeling pity on him and assuming he was mute, strangers sometimes bought his pieces.

One day, the King of Persia was visiting the market in disguise.

Pointing to one of the sculptures, he asked how much it was. The miser acted out a number with his hands.

'I'll give you a quarter of that,' said the king.

The miser shook his head, jumped up and down, and chased the customer away.

A few days passed, and the king was sitting in his counting house when he thought of the miser.

Curious as to why people behaved as they did, he sent his vizier to ask about the miser who made sculptures out of wood.

'He's the meanest man that ever lived,'
said one man.
'He would sell his own mother for a penny,'
said another.

‘He has such tremendous greed,’ said a third,
‘that he would do anything for a purse of gold.’

The vizier's report came back that evening while the king was seated in his throne room. 'Would do *anything* for a purse of gold?' echoed the monarch. 'Could that really be true?'

Wiping a hand over his mouth in reflection,
the king had an idea.

He ordered the vizier to go to the
treasure vaults and ask the treasurer
for a small bag of gold.
'Bring it here,' he said, 'and bring
me the miser as well.'

An hour later, the miser was escorted into the throne room, his eyes wide from being dazzled with real opulence for the first time in his life.

Pinching himself, he wondered whether he was dreaming. But he wasn't, and he knew he wasn't because the king was standing before him, and he was holding a purse brimming with golden sovereigns.

‘Hello,’ said the king graciously.
Squinting an awkward smile, the miser
couldn’t bring himself to speak
– not even for his king.

‘Do you recognize me?’ asked the monarch.
The miser nodded and the king rattled
the large purse.
‘Can you hear what this is?’

Salivating, the miser nodded all the more. 'Well, I will give it to you,' said the king. 'On one condition.'

The miser shrugged his shoulders expectantly.
'On the condition that you can turn
from the meanest to the most generous
man in the kingdom.'

The monarch stepped forward and placed a gold sovereign on the miser's palm. 'Feel it,' he said, 'enjoy the sense of having pure gold on your skin.'

The miser closed his eyes, his short fingers cupped around the coin. He breathed in deeply, perspiration beading on his brow.

'You have one week,' said the king,
'after which time I will myself judge
whether the leopard has changed his spots.'

The gold coin was wrested from the
miser's grasp, slipped back into the purse,
and returned to the treasure vault.

The next thing the miser knew, he was home in his hovel. All he could think about was the piece of gold and the king's offer.

At first he spat at the thought of it – of becoming generous. But as the afternoon wore into evening and into night, the miser felt his toes tingle.

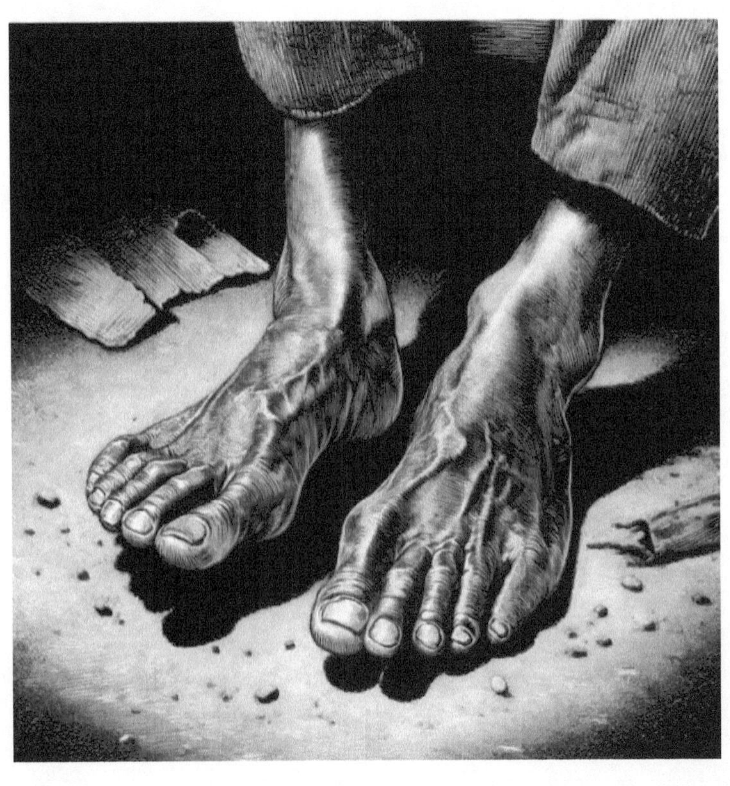

And tingling toes meant only one thing
– that he had to do anything and everything
to get his hands on the gold.

The next day, long before the sun had risen, the miser set off for the market with his sculptures carved from scraps of wood.

Arranging the pieces on the stall,
he stepped back and waited.

Very soon, a wealthy-looking man
approached him and asked the price
of the largest of the sculptures.

The miser did as he always did…

He acted out a high price and stuck his nose in the air arrogantly when the customer attempted to bargain.

But remembering the gold sovereigns,
the miser agreed grudgingly to the customer's
price with a taut, angry flick of the head.

Another buyer arrived a little later,
and another, and a fourth.

Each one was sold the sculptures at a discount.

That night, as the miser was counting and recounting gold sovereigns in his sleep, there was a knock at his door.

Waking from his slumber, he found his neighbour at the door, asking to borrow a quilt.

The miser screwed up his face and slammed the door shut. Then, remembering the gold coin, he unbolted the door and called out through gritted teeth:
'Neighbour, dear neighbour! Do come back!'

The quilt was handed over, and the miser went to bed vexed at having to be generous.

Surprised that the miserly neighbour had agreed to lend him anything at all, the neighbour dropped in the next day with a plan.

‘Where’s my quilt?’ snapped the miser. ‘Oh,’ the neighbour replied, ‘I will bring it back to you later in the day. My guest is using it and he still hasn’t woken up.’

The miser gritted his teeth once again.
He was about to grunt an obscenity
when the neighbour said:

‘Our guests are staying longer than expected. Could we borrow your dining table and chairs?’

Remembering the gold sovereigns,
the miser had no choice but to agree.

After that, another neighbour caught wind of the miser's change of heart and dropped in as well.

'Dear friend,' he said, 'could I borrow your bed, because my in-laws have just arrived. You know how it is…'

The miser was again about to snarl,
but the thought of the coins dazzled him.
'Take it away,' he winced.

For an entire week, the miser struggled to prove he was as generous as anyone else. He had lost most of his few possessions and was the butt of a hundred local jokes.

After seven days, the king's guard arrived at his home and dragged him to the palace.

Finding himself in the throne room once again, the miser dusted himself down and dabbed a kerchief to his brow, hoping to quell the stream of perspiration.

The king arrived. In a foul mood,
he had forgotten about the appointment.
'Who are you?' he growled.

‘I am the man who was just a week ago regarded as thrifty,’ the miser said unctuously.

The king frowned, scratched a set
of manicured nails through his hair.
'Ah, yes,' he said. 'The meanest
man in all the land.'

The miser held up a finger.
'*Formerly* the meanest,' he corrected,
'but now the most generous man there
is, except for you, Majesty.'

‘How can you prove it?’
asked the monarch.

'Well, Your Majesty,' the miser said, 'I sold my sculptures for next to nothing, and lent one neighbour a quilt and my table and chairs, and another borrowed my bed for his mother-inlaw. I have actually spoken to people as well, just as I am speaking to you now – most certainly a reflection of my change of heart.'

The king thought for a moment.
'What can you give *me*?' he asked.

The miser froze.
He was shabby at best, and nothing he owned was even remotely suitable for royalty. Gulping, he fell to his knees and kissed the monarch's signet ring.

‘I give you myself, Your Majesty,’ he said.

The ruler considered the situation,
then he grinned.

'That is indeed an act of supreme generosity,' he said. 'But how will you know what I plan for you?'

Sensing a pang of pain in his gut,
the miser shook his head.
'I would never hope or expect to know,'
he replied meekly.

Again, the king smiled.

He clicked his fingers and a salver was borne through the throne room at chest height. Upon it was the purse filled with gold sovereigns.

'You have earned these,' he said. 'But now you are mine, you will be my court storyteller. Can you tell stories? I hope so, for your sake. Fail me and I'll have your tongue cut out!'

Pawing his fingers through the coins,
the miser nodded.
'Oh yes, Your Majesty, I can relate
the strangest tales ever told.'

'Well, don't dilly-dally,' said the king,
'tell me one now.'

'I have a story to tell,' the miser began obsequiously, 'a story about a miser who, by the gracious wisdom of a most benevolent king, learnt generosity…'

Finis

About the Author

Descended from a long line of storytellers, writers, and savants, Tahir Shah is one of the most prolific authors of his generation. He has published more than sixty books in numerous genres, including travel, fiction, and fantasy, as well as tales for children.

Raised in the tradition of Eastern 'teaching stories', Shah is passionate about stories and storytelling. He regards the ability to learn from folklore as being in us all, what he calls a 'default setting of humankind'. As well as having written scores of books, Shah has made documentaries for National Geographic TV and The History Channel. He is the founder and CEO of the charity, The Scheherazade Foundation.

Books By Tahir Shah

The Writer's Craft

The Reason to Write

Workbook: Comprehensive, Volume I & II

Workbook: Fantasy, Volume I & II

Workbook: Fiction, Volume I & II

Workbook: Historical Fiction, Volume I & II

Workbook: Teaching Stories, Volume I & II

Workbook: Travel, Volume I & II

Novels

Jinn Hunter: Book One – The Prism

Jinn Hunter: Book Two – The Jinnslayer

Jinn Hunter: Book Three – The Perplexity

Hannibal Fogg and the Supreme Secret of Man

Casablanca Blues

Eye Spy

Godman

Paris Syndrome

Timbuctoo

Midas

Zigzagzone

Nasrudin

Travels With Nasrudin

The Misadventures of the Mystifying Nasrudin

The Peregrinations of the Perplexing Nasrudin

The Voyages and Vicissitudes of Nasrudin

Nasrudin in the Land of Fools

Travel

Trail of Feathers

Travels With Myself

Beyond the Devil's Teeth

In Search of King Solomon's Mines

House of the Tiger King

In Arabian Nights

The Caliph's House

Sorcerer's Apprentice

Journey Through Namibia

Teaching Stories

The Arabian Nights Adventures

Scorpion Soup

Tales Told to a Melon

The Afghan Notebook

Daydreams of an Octopus & Other Stories

The Caravanserai Stories

Ghoul Brothers

Hourglass

Imaginist

Jinn's Treasure

Jinnlore

Mellified Man

Skeleton Island

Wellspring

When the Sun Forgot to Rise

Outrunning the Reaper

The Cap of Invisibility

On Backgammon Time

The Wondrous Seed

The Paradise Tree
Mouse House
The Hoopoe's Flight
The Old Wind
A Treasury of Tales
The Tale of Double Six
The Forgotten Game
King of the Jinns
The Destiny Ring
Changing the World
Cat, Mouse
Frogland
Mittle-Mittle
Capilongo
The Princess of Zilzilam
The Singing Serpents
The Tale of the Rusty Nail
The Unicorn's Tear
The Clockmaker Who Travelled Through Time
The Fish's Dream
The Man Whose Arms Grew Branches
The Most Foolish of Men
The Shop That Sold Truth
Qwerty
Renaissance
The Man With the Tiger's Head
The Kingdom of Blink
The Wisdom of Celestine
Dream Soup
The Skeleton Factory
An Unexpected Gift

The Problem Exchange
The Pharaoh Code
The Monkey Puzzle Club
Liquid Time
Cat Dog, Dog Cat
Princess Pickle's Laugh

Anthologies

The Anthologies: Africa
The Anthologies: Ceremony
The Anthologies: Childhood
The Anthologies: City
The Anthologies: Danger
The Anthologies: East
The Anthologies: Expedition
The Anthologies: Frontier
The Anthologies: Hinterland
The Anthologies: India
The Anthologies: Jinns
The Anthologies: Jungle
The Anthologies: Magic
The Anthologies: Morocco
The Anthologies: Nasrudin
The Anthologies: People
The Anthologies: Quest
The Anthologies: South
The Anthologies: Taboo
The Anthologies: Teaching Stories
The Clockmaker's Box
The Tahir Shah Fiction Reader
The Tahir Shah Travel Reader

Research

Cultural Research

The Middle East Bedside Book

Three Essays

Edited by

Congress With a Crocodile

A Son of a Son, Volume I

A Son of a Son, Volume II

Screenplays

Casablanca Blues: The Screenplay

Timbuctoo: The Screenplay

A REQUEST

If you enjoyed this book, please review it on your favourite online retailer or review website.

Reviews are an author's best friend.

To stay in touch with Tahir Shah, and to hear about his upcoming releases before anyone else, please sign up for his mailing list:

http://tahirshah.com/newsletter

And to follow him on social media, please go to any of the following links:

http://www.twitter.com/humanstew

@tahirshah999

http://www.facebook.com/TahirShahAuthor

http://www.youtube.com/user/tahirshah999

http://www.pinterest.com/tahirshah

https://www.goodreads.com/tahirshahauthor

http://www.tahirshah.com

www.ingramcontent.com/pod-product-compliance
Lightning Source LLC
Chambersburg PA
CBHW030522310726
48979CB00010B/1765/J

* 9 7 8 1 9 1 5 8 7 6 1 0 2 *